HOME AT LAST

HOME AT LAST

Mauro Magellan

HUMANICS CHILDREN'S HOUSE
Atlanta, Georgia

Humanics Children's House
P. O. Box 7447
Atlanta, Georgia 30309

First Printing 1990

Library of Congress Cataloging-in-Publication Data

Magellan, Mauro.
  Home at Last/by Mauro Magellan.
        p. cm.
  Summary: Lego the worm searches for a new home and eventually finds one with the help of some animal friends.
  ISBN 0-89334-119-3
  (1. Worms-Fiction. 2. Animals-Fiction. 3. Dwellings-Fiction.)
  I. Title.
PZ7. M27234Ho   1989
(E)-dc20   89-19994   CIP

Printed in Hong Kong

For Marta, Monique and Marc-Gabriel

The Rain, The Road, and The Ants

As more and more clouds moved in, Lego became more and more worried. Lego, by the way, is a worm who lives on a leaf.

When the weather is bright and sunny, his leaf isn't a bad place to live, not to mention a pretty good meal, too. But when it rains (like it's about to do now), Lego is always washed out of house and home.

"I'm not going through this again," he said, looking up at the sky. And that very same day he decided to look for a new home.

Lego knew just where to begin. He packed his little old suitcase with his few things and in no time he was ready to go! Of course, Lego had no idea which way to go.

"It really doesn't matter," he said, "it all leads to one place...home." By noon the next day, Lego came to an old log. It looked like a nice place. Many ants were living there already, but just the same there seemed to be lots of room.

"I think this is it," he said happily, "I'll never be lonely here." He unpacked his few things from his little old suitcase and immediately set out to meet his new neighbors.

3

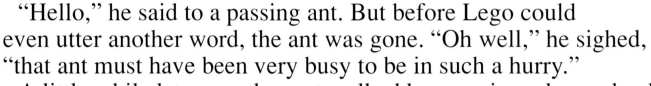

"Hello," he said to a passing ant. But before Lego could
even utter another word, the ant was gone. "Oh well," he sighed,
"that ant must have been very busy to be in such a hurry."
    A little while later, another ant walked by carrying a heavy load.

"Hello," Lego said again, as friendly as he knew how.

"Good afternoon," the ant replied without stopping.
This time Lego walked along side the ant and asked,
"Heavy load?"

"It is," the ant answered.

"Nice weather for flowers, isn't it?" Lego pressed on.
"It is."

"I just moved here, I'm your new neighbor."

"I see."

"My name is Lego. What's yours?"

"I'm ant number 435, east division."

4

"Oh, I'm pleased to meet you," Lego said not sure of the ant's way of thinking. "This is a very nice place you live, isn't it? Did you and your friends make all these tunnels?"

"I'm not authorized to release that kind of information."

It was no use, ant number 435 and every other ant Lego tried talking with had the same personality.

"Oh well," he sighed, "who needs hundreds of friends anyway? And besides, I like quiet evenings at home by myself."

But Lego soon found that a quiet evening at home was as hard to come by as a conversation with an ant. The clanging and clatter of heavy construction all day and all night was more than he could take.

So, after many sleepless nights, Lego decided that the busy side of town was not for him at all.

The Overnight House

Early the next morning, Lego packed his few things in his little old suitcase and once again was on his way to look for a new home. He traveled far that day, and by nightfall he had become very tired. Under the moon, stars, and some tasty grass, Lego fell fast asleep.

7

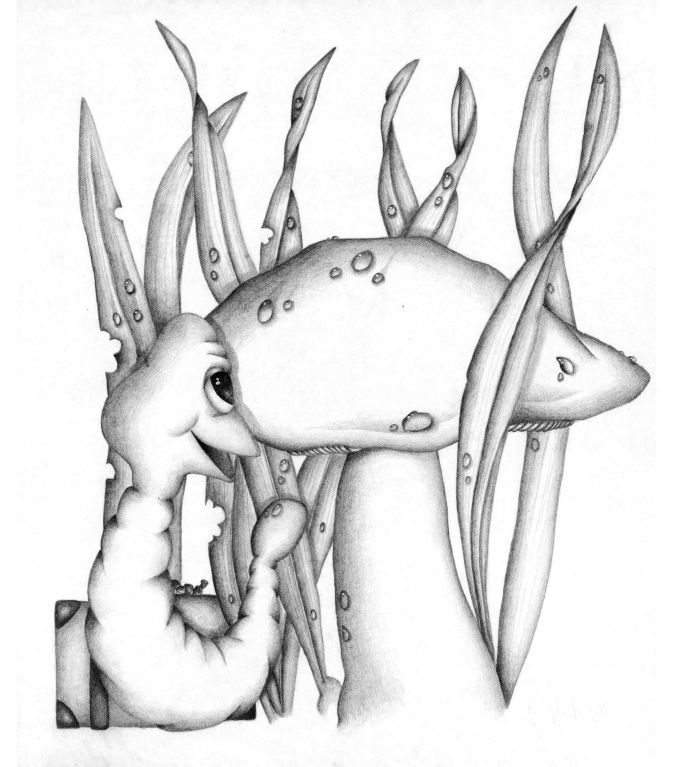

When he woke up the next morning, he couldn't believe his eyes. Out of nowhere, or so it seemed, a big mushroom had appeared.

"Funny, I didn't notice that last night," he said excitedly. "I must have been very tired not to have seen it, or I would have moved right in. I think this could be it!"

The mushroom did seem like a perfect home, rain or shine. That night Lego went to sleep very happy to have found a home, finally. But the next morning something quite surprising happened.
Lego's new home didn't look very new anymore. In fact, it didn't look like anything at all! It was gone. And once again, Lego packed his little old suitcase and sadly went on his way, still in search of a new home.

The Mobile Home

It seemed so long ago since Lego had left his leaf. One day here, another day there. Not belonging anywhere made him very unhappy.

"Maybe a leaf isn't such a bad home after all," he said as he sat down for a rest, "especially if I move someplace where it hardly ever rains, like the desert."

"You don't want to live there, do you?" a voice said from behind him.

"What! Who said that?" Lego cried. He turned his head from side to side but saw no one.

"I'm over here, behind you," the voice continued. Slowly it came out, whatever it was. Out from a shell!

Very surprised, Lego asked, "Is that your house you're wearing?"

"Yes, I guess you can say that," it answered in a friendly way.

"I thought your house - I mean - I thought you were a rock."

"No, I'm a snail. But sometimes my shell does feel like a rock."

"At least you have a home."

"You don't have a home?" the snail asked. He seemed very worried.

"No," said Lego sadly.

"Is that why you want to move to the desert?"

"Yes, but that's a long story."

"Why don't you tell me then, I've got lots of time."

Lego told the snail the whole story in detail, but after he was through the snail still seemed confused.

"I don't understand," he said. "Why are you going to all that trouble? Why don't you just live in an apple?"

"Apple? What's an apple?" Now Lego was confused.

"You don't know what an apple is? I though all worms were smart and read a lot," the snail said a little harshly.

Lego felt foolish. He really didn't know what an apple was.

"I'm sorry," the snail said. "I know all worms are not alike. In fact, everybody thinks all snails are slow and sluggish. That's not true, either. I know a young snail or two who are really quite fast. They don't even carry their shells with them. I know you're not like every worm, but I do believe an apple would make a perfect home for you."

Lego thought about it. And after listening to the snail's thorough description of an apple, he agreed. "Yes, an apple sounds perfect! Where can I find one I can live in?"

"Oh, just about anywhere. They grow on trees."

"THEY GROW ON TREES?" Lego shouted so loud the snail almost jumped out of his house. "Did you really say trees?"

"Yes, I really did say trees. And you're in luck! This is just the right season for them."

Lego couldn't believe his ears. He had heard of money growing on trees, but apples? No, that sounded too good to be true. (You wouldn't easily believe a house could grow on a tree either, even if you saw one.)

"Where can I find an apple tree?" Lego asked. "Is there one nearby?"

"Yes, there's a tree not too far from here. Just follow the road down a bit. You can't miss it, it's the only tree in the middle of the meadow."

"An apple tree?" Lego asked.

"Yes, an apple tree," the snail answered with a smile.

"With apples?"

"Yes, lots of them."

"Thank you very much!" Lego said happily.

"Hey, you know something?" he just realized, "I don't even know your name."

"My name is Les. Les Cargo. I'm pleased to meet you. And what's your name?"

"Lego, just plain Lego. I'm pleased to meet you, too, Les Cargo. You were a big help to me. Thanks again and goodbye, Les!"

"And goodbye to you, Lego. I hope to see you again!" he called as Lego went down the road.

Home At Last

By late afternoon Lego felt as if he had been traveling for a long time. Suddenly, a terrible thought struck him.

"What if Les Cargo was only joking about those apples growing on trees? No, it couldn't be. I've never heard of snails being jokers. But then again, not all snails are alike, and he said that himself!" It was no use, Lego began to cry openly right where he stood.

But he wasn't alone. A big green frog was sitting there watching him the whole time.

"What's wrong?" the frog asked.

"Everything," Lego answered while he was still sobbing.

"Is there anything I can do to help?" the frog asked.

"I doubt it," Lego answered rather impatiently

"How can you be so sure I can't help you?" the frog pressed on.

"Because I want what does not exist."

"What do you want?"

"A home."

"Homes exist."

"For snails they do."

"For snails? What do you mean?" The frog seemed confused.

"That's just what I mean. Homes exist for snails and frogs and everyone else. Except me."

"Why not for you?" the frog asked.

"Because apples don't grow on trees. In fact, apples don't grow at all! They simply don't exist."

"Maybe in the North Pole they don't, but they certainly do here. I just passed a apple tree down the road a little bit."

Lego didn't know what to think. Could this place be full of jokers?

"You know," the frog continued, "I thought worms were supposed to be smart and -"

"I've heard that already," Lego interrupted, "So, you really did see an apple tree?"

"Yes," The frog smiled.

"With apples?"

"Yes, lots of them!"

Lego thanked the frog at least a hundred times and was once again on his way in search of a home. By nightfall, he saw for himself that there really was such a thing as an apple tree. He found one with branches filled with shiny red apples. Lego gripped his little old suitcase tightly and began to climb, searching for the perfect apple that would make the perfect home. Up and up he went, climbing out on a branch.

When Lego looked up, he saw a beautiful red apple. He said happily, "I know this is it. I'm home at last!"

Questions For the Young Reader

1. What kind of animal is Lego, and why does he need a new house?

2. Why did Lego decide not to live in the neighborhood of the ants?

3. Who was the snail that Lego met? What did the snail suggest to Lego?

4. Sam, the Frog, gave Lego directions to find a new house. Where did he tell Lego to look?

5. When Lego finally found a home, what was it? What is the difference between a house and a home?